BLOOD IN THE MAZE

CAROLINE CLARK

HTTP://CAZCLARK.COM

BLOOD IN THE MAZE

"Shadows of a thousand years rise again unseen,
Voices whisper in the trees, "Tonight is Halloween!""
∼ Dexter Kozen.

* * *

**Never miss a book. Subscribe to Caroline Clark's newsletter for new release announcements and occasional free content including this book:
http://eepurl.com/cGdNvX**

* * *

CHAPTER 1

31st October, 2014

Maize Maze

Yorkshire

England

9:59 p.m.

CHRIS WALKED past the pretty girls and felt his feet stumble. Why was it always like this for him?

It didn't matter. This night would be just as bad as the rest unless he did something different. That's what his mother had told him. *Grab the day* or something like that. Take charge of your own destiny and he had decided. It was time he did it. Tonight, this Halloween party was the start of a new him.

The pumpkin costume didn't help. The tough latex made it hard to walk and he was ungainly at the best of times. He knew he looked ridiculous. It would maybe have been cute if he was six, but now!

The giggles from behind him were like little peck, peck, pecks at his nerves. They could be about anything, but inside his costume paranoia ruled, sweat formed on his face and beneath his armpits. It had only been yesterday when he was called Fatty and now he was wearing this great lump of a costume.

Why had he come?

Puppy fat his mum called it, but at thirteen he just wished it would go away and that he could be cool like the other boys, or at the very least accepted. There was one other person in his year who he felt close to. Jennifer. She had moved to the area just six months ago and was always alone. Some of the kids called her snooty but all he saw was a free spirit, a fellow lone survivor battling bravely through this foreign and dangerous world.

She never seemed to care. He had been watching her for a while now. Sat on the edge of things with her head in a book and headphones on to drown out the world. She was pretty. Not as pretty as Poppy Marshal, but just the thought of talking to her filled him with a warmth he couldn't explain. She was the reason he was here tonight. Usually when his mum sent him to these things he would go hide in the woods until they were over and then go home and pretend he had a good time.

Not tonight though, then it came to him. *Seize the day. Carpet Du-um, or something like that.*

A raucous burst of laughter ripped through his thinking. It sounded just like a raven he had seen this morning. Perched on a carcass, it was about to rip out the entrails of a rabbit squashed on the road. It stared at him with one lifeless black eye and cawed at him, *keep off, its mine.* Just like the laughter it made him cringe as he waddled towards a great log fire that burned behind a fence, surrounded by all his classmates.

It looked so welcoming, only he was once more out of place. The boys were dressed as mummies, vampires, zombies, the girls as nurses, vampires and more zombies. They were cool and looked so real that he felt his stomach flip at the eyeball hanging on Jed's face.

Then there was his nemesis. The boy who had pushed him over nearly every day of the last school year. Bradley was dressed as the Grim Reaper and he held the plastic scythe, slicing it through the air as if it were a real weapon.

Chris dropped his head and turned, hopefully he would not be noticed. He almost laughed. Here he was in the gaudiest and most ridiculous costume. It was impossible to not be noticed.

Then he saw her. Holding a hot dog and drinking out of a glass that looked like a skeletal hand. Jennifer. She was wearing a ghost outfit that was nice but clearly homemade. It separated her from the rest of the crowd and endeared her to him even more. This was it. This was his opportunity.

Before the teachers started on the countdown, he

could go over there and ask her to walk through the maze with him. He could do it!

Sweat trickled down his back and he stopped on the spot. One foot poised as he wanted to go forward and yet he wanted to run. His stomach flipped again and hope pulsed through him as he heard his mother's voice.

"You can have anything you want, just go for it. I believe in you my baby boy."

How he wished he had stopped the conversation before the last bit but she was right. He could do this. After all Jennifer looked uncomfortable and alone, she would be glad of a friend.

Long moments passed and the world slowed down. The bright spotlights all pointed at Jennifer. Surrounding her in a halo of luminescence as he dithered on the spot. The laughter and buzz of conversation cocooned him. Excluding him, but for some strange reason it spurred him on. Forward, his foot inched as he imagined her saying yes. Back it drew as another burst of laughter broke into his world, the fire crackled making him leap on the spot.

"Oh dammit," he muttered and pushed himself forward. Forcing his stiff legs to move and lifting the pumpkin slightly.

Each step toward her was like running a race. By the time he stood within two feet of her brightness and looked down into her beautiful brown eyes he was panting and out of breath.

"Hey," he managed.

She looked up from the hot dog and had a touch of tomato sauce on the side of her lip. Part of him wanted to laugh, another part wanted to lick it off and he almost let out a groan.

The seconds passed between them and she said nothing but dropped her eyes as color flushed across her cheeks.

Should he turn and run?

No, he was here and he was about to do some seizing.

"I know this costume is really stupid," his words rushed out so quickly and he saw her eyes widen, did she think he meant hers?

"My mum picked it out for me and I had no choice about wearing it. You know mums." He shrugged his shoulder and the pumpkin bounced around him. Did he see a flicker of a smile on her face?

"Your costume is great. I love you... it... the goul... ghost costume you're wearing. Will you walk with me... around the maze... that is not just with me? If you want some company. It can get pretty scary out there" Oh God he had to shut up or slow down or say something coherent.

She smiled this time, and the noise of the children all died away. She smiled at him and she was going to say yes.

A firm hand slapped onto his shoulder and he fell forward, going down onto his knees at her ankles, before being hauled back onto his feet.

"So, piggy pumpkin is frightened of the maze is he?"

Chris twisted to see Bradley leering at him. The black make-up on his face made him look like death himself.

Chris looked at Jennifer, for a moment her face was one of shock but then it changed into a smile. "He wants me to hold his hand on the walk," she said before dropping her eyes as color shot across her cheeks.

Those words from her were like a punch to the gut and he staggered back into Bradley.

"Urgh, get away you freak." Bradley shoved him hard, unable to move his legs fast enough to regain some balance he tripped and landed in a pile format the feet of the little group.

Slowly he pulled himself to his feet, keeping his head turned away to hide the tears that had formed in his eyes.

Why did he come tonight?

Why did he think things could change?

Head down, he staggered away. He would do his normal, go get some sweets and hide in the woods until the night was over and he could go home. With what felt like wooden legs, he walked away.

Something hit him hard across the back of his knees, below the latex of the pumpkin and he let out a yowl of pain as he leaped forward.

"Hey, stop it." He turned to see Bradley coming towards him swinging the plastic scythe. Only in his mind it was real and it tore through the air singing a song of death as it came for him.

Back and back he stepped until he was out of the lights and into the edge of the corn.

It wasn't time. Mr. Pearce should have been watching. Where was he? All these thoughts went through his head as the Grim Reaper followed him into the corn swinging his scythe so hard that when it hit Chris it felt like it cut to the bone.

The sweet corn towered above him and rattled as he touched it. Like a thousand voices it chased him further into the maze and further away from help.

Death was chasing him, and he ran. Crying and desperate for breath he raced for his life as the Reaper behind him screamed with laughter.

Chris knew he had to escape, he ran for all he could to put a little bit of distance between him and the fiend that chased him, but it was getting harder. It was so hot inside the heavy latex pumpkin and his breath was coming in desperate gasps.

He had to hide, but where?

The corn scared him. It always had, for it could hide so much. The rows all tall and regimental, and yet the corn was ragged and tatty and reached out to grab him. It was so hard to breathe now and he knew he had no choice.

Quickly he pushed himself through the corn and started to move away from the path. It was something he was not supposed to do. But he had no choice. It rattled and slapped at him. Seemed to talk and whisper. To chase him and to call back at his pursuers as it rustled, but he pushed deeper and deeper until it closed in behind him. At last he crouched down and waited.

Suddenly the corn burst apart and The Reaper appeared over him. A pain seared through Chris's chest. Ripping open his heart and forcing it up into his throat. He was sure he had been stabbed and fell backward. Tumbling through the rattling and scratching corn he burst out of it and back onto the path. The Reaper erupted through the corn and swung at him. Chris ducked but it was too late the scythe hit him in the chest and he was pushed over until he landed on his butt. Pain shot through his spine but before he could react he was smashed in the face with the scythe.

His nose broke and blood flew, but his head was tumbling backward and a dull pain was followed by a terrible crack. For a moment the lights went out and he relaxed. It was time to sleep.

Chris woke face down. Mud and twigs scratched across his face and neck and filled his nostrils forcing him to cough and choke. A stone hit his teeth and he screamed but it was no good. He was being dragged, face down through the corn.

Death had him in its grip, and he felt his heart stop for a moment. *Was this it? Was he to die tonight?*

No, his newborn self-cried, but he was so tired. Something warm and wet soaked into the top of his head and ran down his neck. All he wanted to do was sleep and he began to let go. Then he was shoved forward, and his face was suddenly in water.

It filled his nostrils and mouth and tasted of dirt and darkness. Chris tried to cough, tried to move his head but the blackness was coming back. The blackness would take him, and fear reared its ugly head but still Chris couldn't move. He dropped back down, face first, into the puddle. The pumpkin costume was comfortable beneath him and as the cold, dirty water filled his lungs, he was filled with a deep burning desire to hurt Bradley.

He would be back.

CHAPTER 2

*3*1st October, 2017

Maize Maze

Yorkshire

England

9:59 p.m.

JONATHAN PEARCE LEANED against the table and tried to look as if he was watching the students. He hated these class parties, especially the Halloween one. It wasn't because of the incident with Chris three years ago. No, it was the noise, the squealing and shrieking of the kids always gave him a headache. Give him a classroom and his own rules and he could cope but here, in the wild, it was more than he could handle.

Then he spotted movement amongst the children. The woman walked with grace and was head and shoulders above most of the attendees. Dawn Norton was like an Amazon warrior as she stalked her prey. Eagle eyes flicked from side to side as she sauntered among the rabble. Then she spotted someone and moved with a speed that defied her beauty. Reaching out with a hand she grabbed hold of a costume and pulled a boy off another. Jonathon was always intrigued with the pecking order amongst the children but Dawn wouldn't have it. She wouldn't allow bullying.

Jonathan felt his lips part as he looked upon the dream of a woman. Taking a sip of his punch he licked his lips and tasted the brandy he had added to his own drink. It would keep the chill at bay and make the night a little more bearable. Just ten more minutes and he could set them going. At least then he could relax a little bit and maybe try and talk to Dawn.

As the minutes ticked past Jonathon found his eyes pulled to Jennifer Higgins in a too cute ghost costume and Bradley Parker dressed in a red suit and wearing horns. He carried a pointed fork. He was the devil. His suspicions put Bradley at the head of the incident three years ago. The boy was rich, entitled, and spoiled. The worst kind of bully but he had changed after that night. Jonathan didn't believe that he was less of a bully. No, that leopard hadn't changed its spots, it had just learned how to use them. The boy had become more cunning.

Higgins looked miserable and she held onto her clipboard as if her life depended on it. Well she'd better. He had made sure that every group of children had a senior to escort them through the maze. There would be no more getting lost and falling over. Not on his watch.

At last it was time and he wandered over to the start line with his fog horn and starting pistol. At a wave of his hand the lights dimmed and the farmyard was plunged into semi-darkness. Hysterical squeals filled the air.

"Hush now."

All eyes turned to him.

"Are we all ready for the ghost walk through the deadly maze?"

Squeals of delight along with a few rude words and a number of boos greeted him. *Kids today*.

"Good. Now be careful, take your time and no pushing. There are a number of hidden treats but none of them are off the path. Listen to the seniors who come with you and if you get lost seniors, use your radios. All ready for a spooky night?"

This time the squeal was deafening and mostly positive. Well it was the best he was going to get.

With a wave of his hand the spotlights dimmed even more but the entrance to the maze lit up. It had been decorated as a giant pumpkin that the kids would have to run through to enter the maze. If only it would swallow them all up then he could retire early and go off to Barcelona like he always planned. If only!

More lights led into the maze. It had been made safer and safer each year. It was so nice in there now he doubted there would be many scares.

Taking one last look at the kids he raised the pistol in one hand and fired, he cut the tape that barred the entrance.

A squeal of delight let out from the crowd and the kids ran into the maze in their dark and grisly costumes. All blood splattered and gory they were like a hoard of zombies on the march.

Jonathan jumped to one side and had to laugh as the seniors tried desperately to keep their own bunch of children together. It had begun and yet Bradley simply sauntered through the pumpkin, his mobile in his hands as he ignored the kids.

* * *

JENNIFER GRABBED hold of three costumes and held the children back. She had a group of five kids. Two of them were timid and were staying by her side. But the others had gotten caught up in the atmosphere and were ready to race into the dark maze. She was not having it. The maze terrified her and she still had nightmares about finding Chris in his pumpkin suit. It had been her fault. She had laughed at him and allowed Bradley to push and chase him into the maze. Though she didn't know for sure, she suspected that Bradley had killed the Chris that night. Whether it was deliberate she didn't know, but she doubted it was just a simple fall as the police suspected.

For a moment she was back in that awful night. Halfway through the evening there had been a torrential downpour. It meant that everyone had flooded back to the farmyard and hidden in the barn. Drinking punch, eating chocolate and hot dogs. She had noticed that Chris hadn't come back but the teachers, Mr. Pearce said he probably went home. She didn't believe it, so she went to his house and checked. When his mother told her he wasn't there she had searched the maze and she had spotted his costume through the corn.

"Jennifer." Sarah, a cute little girl in a princess's costume was staring up at her. "Can we go before all the chocolates have been taken?"

"Of course," Jennifer said and taking the girl's hand she led them into the maze. It wasn't long before a plastic skeleton swung out at them and the children shrieked with delight.

Jennifer patted their heads as they clung to her and

then she steered them toward the bucket at the skeleton's feet. It was filled with chocolates and little plastic spiders. Delighted giggles replaced the shrieks and the children reached into the bucket. Just as they did Jennifer could have sworn that one of the spiders moved. That it was real and those thick hairy legs were crawling towards the children. Pain sliced into her chest and she leaped forward but the vision was gone, and she could see that it was just plastic. What was wrong with her?

As she turned and lead the children away, a big black spider appeared out of the chocolate. Its eyes staring after them before it skittered from the bucket and into the maze.

CHAPTER 3

*S*ophie jumped back as the grisly skeleton sprang out and danced in front of her face. Goosebumps rose on her arms and a scream froze in her throat. Causing a lump there that stopped her breath. Her lungs ached and her legs were shaking so hard that her knees hurt.

Why had she come on this stupid ghost maze, and how had she been separated from Alice and put in this group with Nathan? The boy was a year older than her and a bully, he scared her almost as much as the darkness.

A shove in her back cleared the block from her throat and she sucked in a breath, coughing and choking as she stumbled forward and bumped into the back of Bradley.

She spun around and her witch's hat fell from her head and the cord caught on her throat. It pulled tight stopping her breath once more and panicked fingers clawed at her throat.

The look Bradley gave her was worse than the skeleton and she skittered back away from him as the rest of the children walked on into the maze. Somehow she freed the cord from her throat and pulled the hat back onto her head.

They came to a stop.

"Which way?" James, an excited boy with a rapt expression on his face asked Bradley.

The older boy took his eyes off his phone for a moment and nodded noncommittally.

Nathan was dressed as a zombie and he grunted as he bumped into Sophie. With a shove he walked past and came up to the junction. It was a crossroad. He peered down each route before pointing to their left. It was the darkest of the routes and Sophie gulped down her panic before looking behind her. Could she make her way back?

Maybe not, they had done at least a dozen turns already and she was scared and disorientated. It would be best to stick with the group and just get this over, but already she could feel tears at the back of her eyes.

Gulping them down she bit her lip to keep the tears at bay and followed along behind the group. Each time they passed one of the floodlights tall shadows loomed over her. As they touched her skin she would draw back all cold and dark inside. It was an awful feeling and she tried to avoid them by keeping close to the edge of the corn.

They passed the severed head, while everyone screamed with delight while she chocked on her fear.

Then they passed a coffin. The children all crowded around to see what was inside but she hung back. Trying to keep the shadows off her skin as they went on down the next path.

Nathan was now at the back of the group. He walked towards her, a mean grin on his face as he waved his arms around and pretended to be a real zombie. The groan he made reverberated inside her chest and rattled her bones as if they were dry and brittle.

Shadows slunk out from his arms and tried to grab her throat but she dived out of their way. Her heart pounded so loud that blood rushed through her ears. *Boom boom, boom boom, boom boom.*

Nathan kept walking pushing her away from the group she skittered back away from him as a scream was ripped from her.

"Keep away," she shouted, but he laughed and just kept coming.

Bradley hadn't noticed and carried on walking with his head in his phone. Sophie slunk even further back until she saw something crawling across the dirt floor.

It was about six inches long and had eight furry black legs. It had to be plastic but then dark, bright eyes turned to look at her and it reared up on its four back legs. Two legs and two awful black fangs waved in the darkness casting huge shadows that danced toward her.

Sophie screamed and ran straight into Nathan.

"Cry baby," he shouted and pushed her to the ground.

Sophie screamed again as she came face to face with the spider only now it was plastic and obviously fake.

Getting to her feet Sophie ran as fast as she could down the path and straight on into the corn. It rattled and flapped around her. Beating at her face and arms as she pushed through. The ears of corn ended in silk that stuck to her face like spiders webs. Panic gave her speed and strength and she raced further into the corn. The elongated styles were hard and dry. They sounded like crinkled paper as they slapped against her shin and curled out like bony fingers to grab onto her clothes and scratch across her face.

Terror was like a demon on her tail and she raced from it, with no thought but run and run until she could run no more. It was only when she burst out into another group of children that she realized she had left Nathan long behind.

"Hey, wait up there," Jennifer said as she pulled Sophie to a stop and then pulled the sobbing child into her arms. "It's okay, it's just make-believe."

Sophie sobbed against the older girl and tried to

explain. "He was chasing me. A zombie and there were shadows, spiders. I want to go home."

"I know, I know," Jennifer said. "You stay with me and we will get you out of here."

Pulling out her radio she turned it on and depressed the mike button. "This is Jennifer Higgins I have found..." she stopped speaking as the radio let out a mighty squeal and then gave nothing but static. Had she busted it?

No matter how she tried, which channel she turned to, or how much she shook it, the radio would do nothing. In despair she turned it off, back on, and off again. They would simply have to walk out of the maze. It shouldn't be too much of a problem. There were some shortcuts that all the seniors knew about.

Taking Sophie's hand she led her further into the maze.

* * *

NATHAN LAUGHED as the little girl in the witch costume quaked before him and then ran. It was the most delicious feeling he had ever experienced.

Quickly he followed her as she darted down the aisle cut into the corn. Turning left and right, she screamed at each plastic skeleton, mummy or severed limb that fell in front of her.

Then she raced straight on at a junction and into the corn. Nathan was going to follow her when a shadow crossed the path in front of him. Fear clenched tight onto his heart and he stopped in his tracks.

What was wrong with him?

There was nothing there just a dark mist that swirled and coalesced in the gloom and yet it filled him with a dread he couldn't explain.

Clenching his teeth he walked toward the corn and the shadow. It formed a more solid shape and a face loomed out of the darkness.

Screaming, he leaped backward and tripped over falling on his back in the mud.

Now he was angry. This was the girl's fault and she would pay for this when he caught her. Only the shadow was coming toward him and it brought with it an icy cold that made his breath mist. The hairs rose on his arms and he jumped up, turned and ran.

The sound of panting and footsteps followed him down the dark and empty aisles of corn. He rounded a corner and came face to face with a skeleton.

He tried pushing the plastic bones to one side, they wrapped around his arm and grabbed at him. He struggled free of its boney grasp and wiped his bloody hands on his shirt.

Blood! There was blood now!

Quickly he ran past the skeleton and on down the aisle. The corn was thicker now, impenetrable. Tears of dread streamed from his eyes, the dust and dirt from the corn stuck to the tears as he felt the buildup of dirt on his face. *No time to wipe it clean, must get away,* he thought. As he neared it the dry dusty styles grabbed for him and he had to slap them away. Pollen rose in the air making him cough. It was as if it wanted to clog his throat and soon he was struggling to breathe.

Had he taken his inhaler tonight?

Laughter was coming from around a corner and he raced toward it. Help would be at hand and he would be safe. He turned the corner to see a dead end. No one was there. Just more and more corn.

Dark black spiders were crawling over the ears, coming for him. Nathan turned to find himself face to face with the evilest pumpkin face he had ever seen.

A black figure was topped with a glowing dark orange head. Vicious teeth leaked blood and a cold light glowed from the eyes.

He hardly noticed the hot urine that ran down his legs as that awful figure backed him toward the waiting spiders.

A heart-wrenching scream was ripped from him only to be drowned out by the noise of one hundred excited, squealing children.

CHAPTER 4

Jennifer kept hold of Sophie's hand as they navigated the maze. The young girl was still shaking, she could tell from the way her shoulders shuddered that she had shed a few tears. What was it with Bradley? Did he never learn his lesson?

Jennifer had hated the boy since the night three years ago when Chris never returned from the maize maze. The death was put down as an accident but she knew different and blamed not only Bradley but also herself. If she had just been nice to him then things could have been so different. Why was it so hard to go against the crowd? To do your own thing?

But it was, both then and now, and she knew that

similar situations played out every day, but that didn't help right now. It didn't make her feel any less guilty. Maybe if she helped Sophie then it was some little step towards her redemption.

They turned a corner and there was Bradley's group. He hadn't even noticed that Sophie was missing. Jennifer did a quick head count and realized another child was missing from the group.

"Bradley, when was the last time you did a head count?" she asked clinging tightly to Sophie's hand as the girl backed away.

Bradley simply sneered.

"You're two missing," Jennifer said.

"What?" Bradley's head snapped up from his phone and he pulled the clipboard from under his armpit.

It was amusing watching him count and Jennifer expected him to get his fingers out at any moment.

"Ahh. Just one now," he said at last coming over to collect Sophie.

"She can stay with me." Jennifer put herself between

the boy and her shaking charge. "Who else is missing and when did you last see them?"

Bradley looked down at his clipboard, ticking down the list with a pencil. "It's Nathan. A nasty little boy he's probably chasing the girls with plastic spiders."

"Use your radio and let Mr. Pearce know."

Bradley pulled his radio from out of his costume and as he turned it on it let out an almighty squeal. He dropped it into the mud at their feet and then gave her a hard stare.

"It's not my fault," she said as she picked it up. The radio was dead. "What about your phone?"

He looked at his phone and shook his head. "No signal. It was working a moment ago."

"We should make our way out of the maze and start a search," Jennifer said.

Bradley was about to argue but she held his gaze with her most stern look and at the last moment he nodded.

"Come on then kids, it's time to go back."

A great moan was let out by all the children but they

dutifully turned and followed them as they made their way out of the maze.

"How long has he been missing?" Jennifer asked.

"It can't be long," he said. "Maybe a couple of minutes. We could always backtrack?"

"Sophie's been with me for ten minutes and she says she was running for longer than that."

"Kid's just a sissy. It may seem long but it wasn't."

They got to the next corner and Jennifer checked her map. It was just a short walk through the corn and they would be out. She turned left ignoring the no-entry signs and the found themselves back in the farmyard.

Sophie's grip on her fingers relaxed as they walked out into the lights. Jennifer searched the waiting children for Nathan. She remembered the boy as he reminded her so much of Bradley. Short spiky hair was jelled to make him look taller and he had a permanent sneer on his face. He was one of the reasons she kept to herself and even now he was causing trouble. For a moment she didn't care. She would just take her charges over to the fire and treat them all to a hot dog. Then she would make sure that Sophie got home.

A scream rang through the night.

Was it just the excited shriek of children having fun or was something out there?

Her eyes searched the crowds but Nathan was nowhere to be seen, and she knew she had to go find him.

* * *

"It's just a mask, it's just a mask, 'it's just a mask," the words fell out of him like a mantra to keep him safe. Like some religious chant he held them in front of him as he backed away from the cold dark evil that had chased him through the corn.

It was darker here. Down a dead-end alley the floodlights could hardly penetrate the tops of the corn and the figure cast a monstrous shadow that lurked over him.

Something skittered across his foot and he looked down to see a spider crawling toward his trouser leg. Shaking it with repulsion his eyes searched all around him. There were spiders everywhere, all moving closer. Coming in toward him as if they were herding him back into the corn.

Dry leaves scratched his back and he swished around batting his hands out behind him. There was nothing but corn. He whipped back to see the pumpkin man grinning.

The face had changed. Now it smiled, and yet that grin turned his blood to ice and took the bones from his legs.

How could it change when it was only a mask?

With quaking knees he moved backward step by step as the spiders and the pumpkin man followed him. The corn closed all around his body grabbing onto him with skeletal and brittle fingers as he rushed back away from the monster.

Monster aren't real.

I'm the one to be afraid of.

What is that thing?

Nathan spun around and ran quickly, batting away the corn, and feeling better now that he was moving.

The maze wasn't that big and if he kept going in a straight line then he would make his way out and that girl would pay. Today, tomorrow or next week. He didn't care how long it took, but she would pay for this. No one scared him and got away with it.

Running was getting harder. The corn thicker and he was soon gasping for breath. He stopped for a moment to listen.

There were no sounds of footsteps, nothing rustled through the corn. He had made it. He was safe.

A squeal of excited laughter and terror came from his right and he headed in that direction.

Maybe he'd fall over, mess up his pants and get Bradley in trouble for losing him. Yeah, maybe he should hide out for a couple of hours. Leave it until they had to come looking for him. Then he could just walk out of the corn like a returning hero and show them how cool he was.

The scent of hot dog drifted on the air along with a slight tinge of smoke. Could his stomach wait that long?

Maybe he could nip out of the corn, grab a hot dog

and then come back and hide. Decision made, he turned away from the sound he had heard and headed where he thought the farmyard would be.

After a dozen or so steps he saw a shadow cross the corn in front of him. Heart pounding he froze on the spot and waited.

Nothing.

Quietly he moved forward but around the suspected spot.

Then he saw the ears of corn bending over to his right. Something black and heavy was weighing them down. What—it was a spider. A huge dark and hairy creature of maybe eight inches across. With eight, inky black, lifeless eyes, it was looking directly at him.

Nathan turned to run but what he saw turned his bowels to ice and his knees gave way as a scream was ripped from his throat.

CHAPTER 5

Jennifer guided Sophie over to a bench where a group of children were sitting around with another senior, Gill.

"Take a seat and stay with Gill," she said and watched as Sophie went and sat next to a girl around her age. *Alice,* she thought. Soon, the two of them were happily chatting and eating from Alice's plate.

"Hey, Gill," Jennifer called. "Can you look after Sophie and my group?" She indicated the other children stood all around her. "Nathan's got lost in the maze and I want to organize a search."

Gill nodded and stood up, immediately taking charge of the children. She was a pretty girl with long brown hair and a serious face, and Jennifer had often wondered if they could be friends.

"That Nathan is a terror. I imagine he's up to no good," Gill said as she shepherded the children onto the benches. "You go, we will all be fine."

Jennifer nodded and headed off to find Bradley and Mr. Pearce.

Bradley was sipping from a bottle of cider at the edge of the food tent. His miserable looking kids were all stood around looking lost.

"Have you found Nathan?" she asked, knowing full well he hadn't even tried.

"The kids just hiding or chasing some girl. Why don't you leave it," Bradley said wiping his lips and coloring slightly.

Jenifer could still hear the scream. Something about it had been different. Primal. It made the hair stand on the back of her neck and her stomach flipped every time it replayed in her mind.

"Remember Chris?" she said.

Bradley spat out a mouthful of cider. The way his

face had turned as white as her costume, she knew he was guilty, but he simply nodded.

Together they walked over to Mr. Pearce, who stood talking to Miss Norton. Jennifer was embarrassed at the looks he was giving the other teacher. It was pathetic. She thought she even saw a little drool at the corner of his mouth.

"Mr. Pearce." She still couldn't make her voice sound less than respectful and she hated herself for being so meek. Hadn't she learned anything in three years?

"What now?" he asked.

"Nathan is missing and I want to organize a search party."

"Well, do you now?" He stood up tall and looked down at her with a sneer that could have rivaled Bradley's, but she wouldn't back down. Not after Chris.

"That boy is trouble I'm sure it's nothing." He started to turn away from them.

"You may be right," her voice was as sharp as a whip crack and he turned back around. "But I still remember Chris going missing, and I won't risk another child being killed in this damn maze."

Shock, worry, and finally a touch of guilt crossed his face, but after just a few seconds he pulled out his radio and twiddled with the dial. Just like the others it let out an ear-splitting shriek. "What is wrong with this?" he asked and waved the radio at them.

"Ours were the same," Bradley said. "Or we could have just arranged a search without you," the disdain in his voice was apparent.

"Watch your tone. Well, we made plans for this. I'll send up the flare. Go to your assigned quarters and work your way through the maze."

Bradley and Jennifer nodded at each other and she thought she saw a touch of respect in the boy's eyes. It brought a smile to her lips as she headed to the right. In the event of a problem and the radio's not working they all had assigned paths to walk. Collecting any stragglers and meeting in the center of the maze before they then walked out on the same routes. It should cover every track and it should mean that no one could be lost.

As she stood before the creepy looking corn it

seemed to whisper to her. The leaves rattled together murmuring and muttering with a dark undertone that challenged her. *There's no getting out*, the leaves said as they slithered together. *No escape*, and she believed them. Somehow she knew that if she went back into that corn that she wouldn't escape. Yet she had to go back. Maybe Nathan was up to no good, and maybe he was hurt. One way or the other she would find him.

* * *

JULIET LET out a delighted shriek as the plastic spider dangled in front of her. Her best friends Lily and Grace shrieked with her and the three girls clung together. They had never been so frightened and had so much fun before.

A firework arching up into the sky. They waited for the pop and the explosion of color but nothing happened. It just hung there like a red star before slowly falling back down.

"Are there to be fireworks Miss Ava?" Juliet asked.

"No, that's a signal for me. Come on now let's get moving." The older girl turned her clipboard over and studied a map. She knew the drill. They had to make it to the center of the maze along a pre-ordained route to collect any children that had got lost.

Ava decided she would make very little fuss about it as they were about halfway through the maze. That way they could enjoy the rest of the walk and still do their job. They got to the next corner and she turned them right. If she remembered there was a guillotine down here that would chop of a head just as they passed. The girls would love it.

A cloud passed over the moon and the maze felt a little darker, a little less friendly but she shrugged the thought away. The floodlights made it easy enough to see and she had a torch in case of emergency. Up ahead she could see the guillotine. It rocked in the wind and then a darkness surrounded it.

Behind her the girls screamed. The sound so piercing it set her heart a racing and raised the hairs on her arms.

As the girls surged forward she saw a shape, a shadow move from behind the guillotine and disappear into the corn. The maize rattled and whispered, but didn't move. It was as if the darkness had gone straight through it.

The girls arrived at the guillotine and the lights dimmed. It was as if the generator was running low on fuel or the bulbs were fading. The girls didn't notice and were crowding around the guillotine waiting for something to happen.

Then dummy leaning over it looked so real, the wooden frame looked real. She reached out to touch it just as the blade fell. There was a sucking and slurping sound as the blade dropped. Warm liquid splashed across her face and she jumped back as a thump heralded the head falling into the waiting basket.

Ava's mouth fell open. She could see the girls in their bright and gory Halloween costumes were covered in blood. It made no sense. Had one of the boys rigged something to cause this?

The sound of thunder jerked her eyes up to the sky. It was getting even darker and rain would soon fall.

"Come on girl's we had better hurry."

As she turned to lead them away she could see

something orange within the corn. The sensible part of her knew she should go check if it was a lost child but there was another part of her that wanted to run.

Like a jack-o-lantern the orange was lit from within. It followed them as they rushed down the rows and whenever she caught sight of it she felt a shiver run down her spine.

CHAPTER 6

Jennifer wished she was not alone. The light drizzle was making it hard to see and her torch kept fading out, but that was not what was bothering her. The maze felt different. There was a threatening vibe that came off it that you could almost see.

A scream rang out to her right. It was visceral and chilling, and sounded more like an adult than a child. It sounded like someone afraid for their lives, someone in pain. Only that made no sense. If a child screamed then it would just be the fun of the night. The maize maze had been designed to both terrify and entertain and many of the decorations were very real. Very lifelike. But the adults knew them all. They knew it was make-believe.

Another scream had her turning to her left. This one rose on the air like an opera singer's big finish and then was choked off like a strangled cat.

Looking right and left, she walked a little further. It was getting muddy underfoot and the ground was slippery. With each step she took, it held onto her shoes, as if it wanted to pull her in. To swallow her whole, but she had to keep going. The sooner she made it to the center the sooner she would be with people. Though she had always been a loner, now she wanted to be in a crowd more than ever. To be surrounded by people, and to never be alone again.

She came to a crossroads and pulled out her map. This didn't seem right, she should have come to a T junction and gone right then another and gone left. Had she gotten onto the wrong route?

If she had then she could be trudging through the maze for hours.

Behind her, the corn rattled and whispered, as if someone... some*thing* was racing towards her. She whipped around but nothing was there.

The tall rows were impenetrable. Like eyeless soldiers they stood in her way. It was hard to pull her gaze from them, to turn her back on them, but another scream insisted she spun around.

When she turned back the crossroads had gone, and she was surrounded by corn.

"No!" she let out the word as a scream of her own.

Like sentinels, corn blocked her way. The flower heads waved with disapproval high above her, the staves rattled, and the stalks made an impenetrable barricade that she could not escape through.

What was she to do?

Spinning round and round she looked for an opening. *It had to be there. Just a moment ago there were four paths leading away, they must be there.* She must just be missing them.

Coming to a stop she dropped to her knees panting and fighting for breath. The wet ground soaked through her trousers and sucked her down.

Where had the road gone?

Biting back tears she tried to think, but there was a shadow in the corn and it was coming this way.

As the shadow moved closer the corn rubbed together and urged it on. It mumbled its approval and murmured its support.

"She's here," it seemed to say. *"I've got her trapped, and will hold her for you."*

Jennifer hauled herself to her feet and stalked around the corn. It held her back, but she could see a light amongst the shadow, almost hiding but wishing to be seen... and she knew it was Chris. He was coming for her, and she deserved it. She had laughed at him. She had unintentionally helped Bradley, and his death was as much her fault as it was the other boys.

For a moment her knees sagged again and she wanted to slump down onto the ground. To let the rain soak her to the skin and to let the shadow with the orange light come and devour her, but she couldn't give up.

A child's scream rose above the rain and the sound of it was like a knife to her chest.

The child was close. Maybe it was in danger and maybe she could help. She wouldn't give in, never would. No one had helped when she was bullied. No one had come to her aid and it could just as easily have been *her* dead in the corn. She would save this child no matter what.

The shadow was getting closer, the rain fell heavier, and the corn looked even more impenetrable.

She rushed the corn. It flapped at her face and the hard stalks grabbed at her but she surged through and raced away from the shadow and towards the scream.

The corn batted at her face, legs, head and clung onto her as she raced through but she would not give in.

Once more the child's scream rose on the wind and she turned towards it. To her right she could see a flash of orange, and she remembered the ridiculous latex pumpkin he had worn. It was the least scary costume she had ever seen and yet that flash of orange drove terror into her heart.

Still, the child was across the shadow's path and she would save him. Somehow she knew it was a boy and she suspected it was Nathan. Maybe Chris was punishing him for being a bully. Maybe he was right but Nathan wouldn't die. Not tonight and not if she could help it.

* * *

Bradley walked down the narrow rows and shrugged his shoulders against the rain. Why had he let them force him into this? It made no sense. It was the last place he wanted to be. The Maze and the Maize both gave him the creeps and nightmares for weeks after he even heard of them.

He'd never told anyone about what happened to Chris. After all these years it should be a distant memory and yet the nightmares wouldn't let up. He had hoped that coming back here a little older, would rid him of the scary dreams, and yet here he was in an even bigger nightmare.

The sound of a scream came from his right. For a moment he started to turn away. If the kid was in trouble then he would be best to keep out of it. Then he saw the shadow. It was just a darkness in the corn and yet it moved like a person. Moved with purpose and it was stalking him.

Bradley moved towards the screaming boy and away from the shadow. He could hear the corn rattling behind him but it was hard to see much. The torch had given up ages ago and the floodlights had dimmed creating long dark shadows within the rows of corn. Did the school buy all cheap equipment, or was something making everything break?

Originally, he had the thought it had been a joke, but suddenly he knew it was true. Something was causing this. A flash of orange appeared within the shadow and it was getting closer. A flash of pumpkin and he knew who was after him. Chris.

Chris was stalking him through the corn and he was after revenge.

The corn rattled and shook, urging on his pursuer, and yet mocked him when he tried to run. The ground was wet and slick now, and he stumbled along with rain running down his face.

Another scream rang through the night and he turned to race towards it. He didn't care who it was. Or how frightened they were, he just wanted to be with another human being. Or at least another alive one.

Bradley arrived at a crossroads and he recognizes where he was. To the left was where he killed Chris. Where he hit him with the plastic scythe. He remembered the way blood had sprayed through the air. He remembered the thrill as the big boy with the massive pumpkin costume had toppled over backward.

Then he had panicked. If Chris had told he could be expelled, and his father was already ready to cut him off. It was too much to risk, so he had grabbed Chris by the ankles and dragged him into the corn. Leaving him there in the hope that he wouldn't be found. His intention was to see him the following day and to scare him into saying nothing only that never happened.

A flash of orange appeared to his right and herded him to the left.

Another scream cut through the air and he wanted to run. He wanted to run back to the fire and then home to his mum. He turned, a shape came out of the corn but it wasn't Chris, at least not anymore.

CHAPTER 7

Jennifer recognized where she was as she came into a clearing within the corn. It was the area where Chris had died. Sitting on a rock was Nathan. His head bowed he wept silently. A lump formed in Jennifer's throat. That very rock was probably the one where Chris hit his head. She knew this was madness. The field would have been plowed and reseeded countless times in the years since that dreadful incident and yet she knew it was. Just off to his left she could see water through the corn.

It would be a puddle, the one where Chris had been dragged. The one where he drowned. Shaking her head she forced her panic down and concentrated on the boy sat weeping.

"Hey, you're okay, you're safe," she whispered as she approached him.

He looked up with big round eyes full of tears. "I'm sorry," he said. "I won't ever bully again."

Jennifer pulled him to her and held him close. She could see cuts and bruises on his face and arms. It looked like the corn or something had given him quite a beating. She hugged him close as they perched on the rock inches above the wet muddy ground in the pouring rain. How she wished she could radio for help or at least let the others know where they were.

"We have to go," Nathan said and he looked up at her, his lip quivering in the rain.

"We will," she said, and helped him to his feet.

As they turned the sound of something crashing through the corn came out of the darkness. The corn rattled and shook in all directions, as if a storm was brewing. It was disorientating and hard to tell where anything was coming from.

Jennifer hugged Nathan tightly and turned around in the clearing. All she could do was try and keep him safe.

The corn parted and Bradley burst into the opening. He dropped to his knees in front of them, panting and gasping for breath. "I never thought I would find anyone," he said as he gasped for air. "There's something in the corn."

"We know," Jennifer said, and Bradley looked up.

"You, and you." He pointed at Nathan. "You little shit, you're the one who got me in this trouble. Come here." He reached out to grab Nathan but Jennifer twisted away.

Nathan shrieked and pulled out of her arms. It happened so fast but he raced across the clearing and was engulfed in a black cloud. Like a rag doll he went limp and she feared that he was dead. A scream caught on her lips as the shadow, the cloud of darkness and despair moved towards her. Held within was the marionette of the little boy in a zombie costume.

Jennifer backed away until she bumped into Bradley.

He shoved her forward and she fell to her knees in front of the darkness.

Jennifer thought that her life was over and she was ready. She would give up for she had failed to save the boy. Once more it was her fault. If she had just clung on tighter then he would still be alive and she would have a reason to fight.

A face formed in the shadow. The face of a jack-o-lantern with the sharpest teeth and the wickedest smile she had ever known and yet there was something familiar about it.

Chris, there was something of the kind boy hidden behind the nightmare.

Light reflected from the eyes and winked in the darkness as the gloom moved forward to engulf her.

"Chris, stop this," she shouted. "Let Nathan go and leave us."

"Nooooo, he deserves to die. You all deserve to die." The voice was wet and guttural and it made the skin crawl on the back of her neck.

"He's just a child and he's learned a lesson," she said pulling herself to her feet she stood her ground.

"I saw what he did to that girl. Felt the delight he felt, I know his kind."

The eyes flashed through the darkness. It was like a candle flame burning only brighter and directed behind her. A black rod of smoke poured out and formed a hand, a sharp, clearly defined finger pointed past her. Jennifer turned to see Bradley. The light reflected in his eyes for a moment and then was gone.

Bradley turned to run but the corn rattled together to form an impenetrable barrier. They really were trapped. This time there would be no escape.

Jennifer's throat was so tight she could hardly breathe. There was a pressure on her chest and she was cold, so very cold. Slowly she turned back to Nathan. The pumpkin head clearer now and she shied away from it. There was also a shape in the darkness. The shape of a man and in his arms was Nathan.

The child's eyes open so wide they looked as if they would pop from his face. He was alive but terrified.

"Be calm, Nathan," she spoke as naturally as she could. "I will get you out of here, I promise."

A cold laugh rustled on the wind. It battered her ears and ripped through to her bones.

"No one is leaving."

The words were like a force of their own, she could hear them and feel the way they resonated across her chest.

The wind picked up and she was almost blown off her feet. But she dug her heels in and raised her head. She was looking straight up into that terrible face and she wanted to flinch, wanted to run but she wouldn't. This was her fault and she would make it right.

"I'm sorry," she said.

The wind died down just a little.

"Sorry," was a whisper through the corn.

"This was all my fault. I was scared of Bradley, scared of all the cool kids, and I was cruel to you to save myself. Never again. I promise you. If you had come to me without Bradley I would have said yes. I nearly did say yes, but I was stupid and afraid."

"I just wanted a friend," the words were a whisper on the wind. "Toooo be looooved."

"I know," she answered turning to where the words sounded all around her. Then she turned back to him. "I wanted the same and I would have been your friend. All I wanted was to fit in and that is the most stupid anyone can be. Who wants to fit in when you can be yourself, unique, just like you were... are."

The wind rose and swirled around her. It rocked her on her feet and she wheeled her arms to hold her ground. She could smell death and decay on that wind and she wondered if that was what waited for her, but it didn't matter. She had to save Nathan, even though he was a bully. She had to save him and to make this right.

"Take me and let the boy's go," she shouted over the wind. "Take me, like you wanted to do that night. Take me."

The wind picked up to such a crescendo that she was knocked off her feet and sent flying backward through the corn. As she landed she hit her head and the world turned darker. It had worked, he was taking her. Killing her, she just hoped that he would honor her deal and that Nathan and Bradley would be set free.

With that thought her eyes closed and the world faded away.

CHAPTER 8

As the wind grew stronger and Jennifer was sent flying across the clearing, Bradley noticed a break in the corn. He didn't even think about helping the others but raced for the exit as fast as his legs could carry him. Once into the corn he ran along the rows as fast as he could. There was no thought of Jennifer or Nathan. No thought of finding help. All he wanted to do was get out of there and never return.

The wind died down and the rain slowed to nothing but a drizzle. On and on he ran until his lungs felt as if they would burst, and his calves burned with fatigue. Why hadn't he found his way out of the maze? It wasn't that big, and he should have cleared it long ago.

Exhausted, he slowed to a walk and looked around him.

To his right was the clearing with that dreadful rock. At one side lay Jennifer and next to her was Nathan. Were they dead?

Turning he ran in the opposite direction. The corn slapped at his face, his arms, and his legs. It constantly battered against him and the muddy ground sucked onto his feet. Soon he was forced to slow down once more. His breath coming in desperate gasps he leaned over to rest for just a moment.

When he straightened up he saw the clearing. He was back in the same place.

"No!" he screamed into the darkness. "No, this can't be."

Turning he tried to run again only this time a dark figure stood in his way. It was surrounded by a glowing light and the head was a hideous pumpkin. The mouth opened and closed as the spirit came towards him. It looked big enough to swallow him whole or to chomp off his head.

Bradley turned and ran to the clearing. Maybe he could get behind Jennifer. Maybe he could use her as protection.

As he entered the clearing he could hear the spirit, Chris, just behind him. As he turned his foot slipped and he fell. Windmilling his arms he tried to break the fall but it was no use. With his heart in his throat, he hit the soft ground and his face fell into the mush.

A stench so bad it caused his hot dog to surge up from his stomach into his nose and mouth, he hauled himself up onto his elbows and let out a scream.

Bradley had realized, it wasn't the ground that he had sunk his face into but the decomposed chest of Chris. He could see white bones sticking through the rotten flesh and bits of orange latex were floating in the soup of the boy's intestines.

Though he knew this was not possible. Chris had been found and buried years ago, it was so real that he could taste the corruption. Feel the flesh melting between his fingers as he scrambled for purchase. For anything to use to push back to his feet.

A terrified scream ripped from him as he spat out the flesh he had inhaled. The scream rose to a higher pitch as he was hauled to his feet and spun around by the pumpkin-headed specter.

Bradley dangled in the air, screaming and shouting for all he was worth before he was tossed aside. Was he being allowed to escape? Getting up he ran and ran through the corn as fast as he could but each time he was exhausted he ended up back at the clearing.

EPILOGUE

Jennifer woke to the sound of shouting. It was still raining and she was cold and wet, but she was alive and nestled against her was Nathan. Slowly she raised her head and looked around her. The clearing was empty. Bradley had gone, and so had the spirit.

She let out a sigh of relief and then shouted into the darkness. "Over here."

Soon, the sound of the corn rattling and rustling heralded a rescue party, but before they appeared from out of the corn, Chris reappeared. For a moment it was the smiling boy that she had once known. He was just a shadow in the gloom and

Jennifer knew he had come to take his prize. Bradley had no doubt run away, he and Nathan would be found, but she would have to go with Chris. It didn't matter, she was tired of the guilt. She would do this to save Nathan.

Jennifer climbed to her feet, stood in front of Chris, and smiled. His face changed and was replaced with the hideous pumpkin head and he reached out and put his hands on either side of her head. It was like her brain was pierced with ice. Shards of cold sliced into her cerebral cortex and she screamed out her pain. Then the pain was gone and she was inside Bradley. She saw his death play out before her and then a voice sounded in her head.

"You are left to tell the tale. Warn others what happens to bullies if they come near me. I leave blood in the maze, but nothing else will be found."

Jennifer dropped to her knees and suddenly the pain and voices in her head were gone, she heard the corn rattle as the rescue party found her.

"What are you doing hiding here?" Mr. Pearce's voice was grating as always.

"Are you for real?" she said, as she grabbed Nathan and following their trail, walked out of the maze.

* * *

IT WAS THREE YEARS LATER, Jennifer sat around a fire at the side of the maze and told her tale to any children that would listen. She had done it every year since that night, and she knew she would do it every year until she died. Maybe in years to come she would sit here alone, but for now she had an eager audience. The kids squealed and oooed as she told her tale. Their eyes full of fear, some full of guilt. She hoped the tale worked. For if it didn't, she knew that Chris would be waiting.

"So," she said. "Bradley dropped to his knees on what seemed like his hundredth visit to the clearing. The terror was every bit as real as the pain in his chest as he fought for breath. But he couldn't go on. Not again, not anymore. Then he looked at the corpse that he had fallen into. The corpse of Chris, the boy he murdered, only it wasn't Chris. This time he recognized the costume. It was a red suit and there were horns on the decomposed head. It was him. He had died in this maze and by the look of it he had died some time ago. He had fallen into his own corpse."

She paused and waited for the excited shouts and squeals to die down and then came her grand finish.

"Once more he began to scream, and this time he thought that he would never stop. Well children listen." She put her hand to her ear and as if on cue the sound of a scream reverberated around the maze. It happened every year. At first, she thought it was just a coincidence, but now she knew different.

"If you come down here at night, especially around Halloween you can often hear Bradley as he screams and runs and then screams some more. So my friend's learn your lesson. Be nice to each other and never bully."

Big eyes stared up at her and the children all nodded their heads. She just hoped that they would listen.

Tommy Hill jabbed Joseph Springs in the ribs and growled. "Don't think a fairy story is going to save your ass from a beating when we get in there wimp."

As Joseph turned to look up into the bigger boys eyes, he thought he saw... no... he was sure he saw, two piercing orange eyes in the darkness.

*** * ***

Halloween is my favorite time of year. There are so many tales to tell, so many spooky places to visit.

DADDY WON'T KILL YOU – PREVIEW

Dusk fell quickly around a lonely, dilapidated cottage. It brought a feeling of depression to the day, as if a dirty blanket was being dropped over something best left hidden. The windless air disturbed nothing and a preternatural quiet surrounded the property. It was almost like the world held its breath, waiting for this moment to pass.

Strangled weeds pushed through a worn path which led from the house and terminated at the road. A crumbling gatepost leaned away from the path, and a tatter of yellow crime scene tape hung forlornly from the pitted concrete. Behind the post, a removal van hulked at the curb. Its carnivorous doors were open and waited hungrily for the remnants of life that it would swallow whole and regurgitate far from here.

A crow cawed, a desperate and lonely sound, from somewhere behind the cottage. The tattered screen door was shoved open by a man in dark overalls. He pushed through with his back, a small table clutched in his hands. Maneuvering around the small door and easing the chair through the frame, he stepped toward the path. Behind him, a second workman exited the house. This one carried a wooden rocking chair, held away from his body as if it was distasteful, unclean. His dark brown eyes flicked from the chair to the cottage and back again, as sweat slowly traced a line down the stubble on his cheek.

He wanted to put it down, to run from here and spend the rest of the night in a scorching shower, but he could not show his fear, and stoically followed his colleague.

The men arrived at the van, and the table was worked into the last remaining space, between boxes, an old-fashioned dresser, a bed, and other furniture that all appeared to come from a different era. Nervous glances passed between them as they realized the rocker wouldn't fit. They looked at the property, silhouetted in the dark, and back at the van.

Sitting on the roof of the cottage, a large, ink-black crow cawed out a challenge. Before the men, the chair rocked on the concrete.

They stepped back, one toward the van, the other away. Both eyed the chair warily. Their job was to clear the property, but darkness was falling and they wouldn't come back.

The first man, the younger of the two, reached behind him and pulled cardboard from one of the packing boxes. With a pen from his pocket, he wrote something on it and placed it in the rocking chair.

The two men laughed, a false, hollow sound, and walked to the front of the van. As they drove away, the rocking chair was shrouded in moonlight. It started to move. Backward and forward, it rocked, despite the stillness of the night.

* * *

A black SUV stood in front of a large townhouse. The paintwork was polished so deeply you could dive into it, but the gloss couldn't hide the rust dotted along the wheel arches, or the scratch on the rear panel. The car was long past new.

The doors were all open and the car looked like a giant beetle, poised pre-flight. In the rear seat, six-year-old Lucy fidgeted against the faded leather. Her angelic face was surrounded by golden curls and lit with excitement as she jiggled in her seat. She wanted so badly for this trip to be perfect, like the trips she remembered, the long walks with Daddy, coming back to the smell of Mummy's pies, and falling asleep on the sofa. She believed that if she imagined it perfect, then that was how it would be.

Next to her, nine-year-old Chase had his head buried in a book about dragons. She knew he had read it over a hundred times, or at least that was how it seemed. Some days he would recite whole passages, roaring like a dragon to make her laugh and squeal with delight. The story was one of his favorites, but she knew he was also deeply excited. He had been reading the same page for the last twenty minutes.

She wanted him to talk, wanted to tell him about the

trip, but he pretended to be engrossed in the story, knowing that it would drive her wild. She wasn't going to let it.

Lucy jiggled again and poked his arm.

He feigned indifference, keeping his eyes down, hidden by wavy brown hair that flopped across his face.

She grabbed for his book, her clumsy fingers slipping from the pages as he pulled it away with a stern expression. Quickly, he looked down, but it was too late. She spotted the smile and it spoiled his ruse.

"You're just teasing," she said, and grabbed for the book again.

Chase pulled it away and lifted it higher. "This is a really good bit."

"Show me." Lucy tried to peer at the page but it was held too high.

At last, Chase lowered the book and closed it with a thump. Then he closed his eyes and lowered his head again, hiding his face.

Lucy watched as his shoulders shook with mirth.

"You're laughing," she said, and thumped his arm.

"Am not."

"I can't wait," Lucy said, giggling with anticipation. "Aren't you excited?"

Chase kept his head down, but the book began to shake as barely suppressed laughter shook his shoulders. He raised his head and stuck out his tongue, which caused Lucy to giggle even more uncontrollably. Folding the book in his lap, he turned in the seat. "A week in a cabin with you … sounds like torture." But his smile told a different story.

Lucy grabbed for the book again and the car was filled with happy laughter.

"Jesus. I'm on the phone." A woman's harsh voice drifted over to the car.

Lucy wilted in her seat, her excitement extinguished like a daisy too close to a flame. She glanced across the garden, toward the front door. The bright colors of the summer flowers were fading. Desperately clinging to life as the seasons began to change. They seemed sad to her and lowered her mood even more.

Find out what happens to this family when

they encounter something old and evil. **Daddy Won't Kill You** is based on the true story of the Dead Man's Chair. Read it now on Amazon http://a-fwd.to/39YGCrP

MORE BOOKS FROM CAROLINE CLARK

Books are FREE on Kindle Unlimited

Never miss a book. Subscribe to Caroline Clark's newsletter for new release announcements and occasional free content: http://eepurl.com/cGdNvX

The Spirit Guide Series:

The Haunting of Seafield House - Gail wants to create some memories – if she survives the night in Seafield House it is something she will never forget.

MORE BOOKS FROM CAROLINE CLARK

The Haunting on the Hillside - Called From Beyond - A Woman in White Ghost Story. A non-believer, a terrible accident, a stupid mistake. Is Mark going mad or was his girlfriend Called from Beyond?

The Haunting of Oldfield Drive - DarkMan Alone in the dark, Margie must face unimaginable terror. Is this thing that haunts her nights a ghost or is it something worse?

* * *

The Ghosts of RedRise House Series:

The Sacrifice Dark things happened in RedRise House. Acts so bad they left a stain on the soul of the building. Now something is lurking there... waiting... dare you enter this most haunted house?

The Battle Within - The Ghosts of RedRise House have escaped. Something evil is stalking the city and only Rosie stands between it and a chain of misery and death.

Suffer the Children – Two young ghost hunters find themselves in a house that will not let them leave.

Standalone Books

<u>Daddy Won't Kill You</u> A rocking chair, relaxing, comfortable, soaked in the blood of its victims. – Based on a true story about The Dead Man's Chair

<u>The Haunting of Brynlee House</u> Based on a real haunted house - Brynlee House has a past, a secret, it is one that would be best left buried.

<u>The Haunting of Shadow Hill House</u> A move for a better future becomes a race against the past. Something dark lurks in Shadow Hill House and it is waiting.

Printed in Great Britain
by Amazon